MADAGASCAR™

MARTY

ALEX

GLORIA

MELMAN

D0102557

Alex the Lion, Marty the Zebra, Melman the Giraffe, and Gloria the Hippopotamus lived at the city zoo. Alex loved performing for the people, but Marty dreamed about going to the wild.

One night Marty escaped from the zoo! And so did the penguins! Alex, Melman, and Gloria were scared for Marty. They looked all over New York City for him.

 circle triangle rectangle sphere cone cube cylinder

NO STANDING

NEWS

Shape Search   Fun Fact   Telling Time   repeat

 Alex, Melman, and Gloria finally found Marty and the penguins at the train station. But the police found them too.

The four friends were put in crates and loaded onto a boat going to Africa. Alex and Marty argued about why they had been sent away from the zoo. Meanwhile, the penguins took control of the ship and steered it toward **Antarctica!**

Alex, Marty, Melman, and Gloria argued so much that their four crates fell off the boat! They washed up on the island of **Madagascar**. The four friends met lots of new animals.

The local **lemurs** were very friendly. They were happy to meet these big zoo animals. The locals tried to make the four friends feel right at home.

GO

Alex, Melman, and Gloria did not like living on the island. But Marty loved it! He built a cozy **cabana.**

Cabana Vowels

Telling Time

repeat

The four friends looked all over the island for people. Finally, they ended up at the great **baobab** tree.

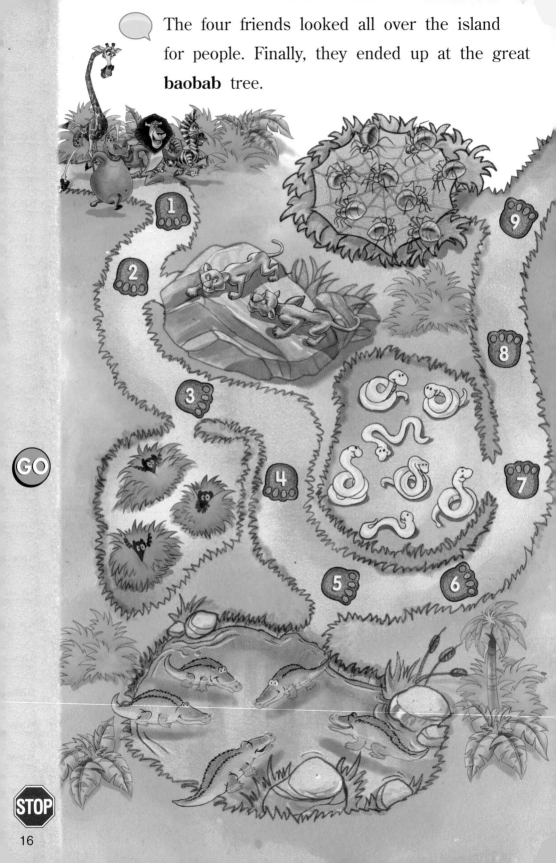

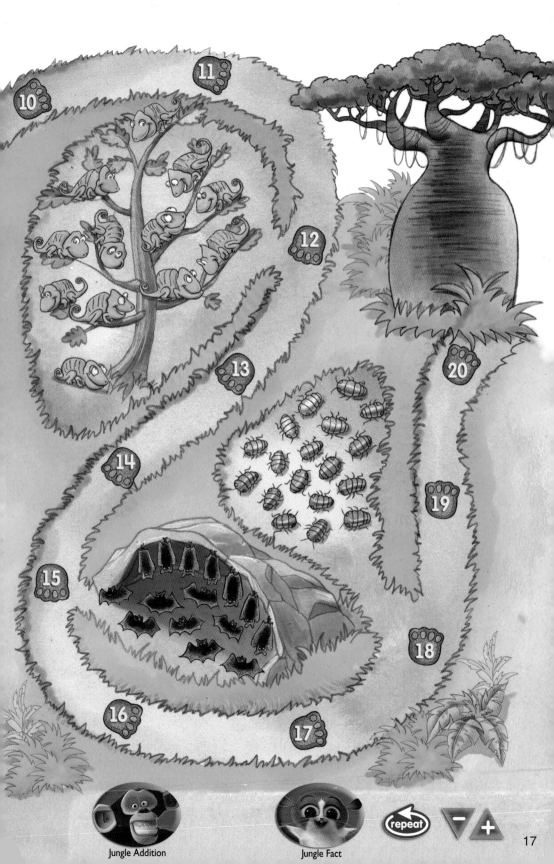

Meanwhile, the penguins found Antarctica. But it was too cold! They decided to go back to Madagascar to get Alex, Marty, Melman, and Gloria.

NOUNS

VERBS

SOUND EFFECTS

Dear Mr. Zookeeper,

You won't believe all the gigantic _____ we've seen in Antarctica. When we got here, they all started _____. Then we shouted _____. After that, the _____ all opened their mouths and inside were hundreds of _____. When they were _____, they made a loud sound like this _____. Wish you were here.

Love,

The Penguins

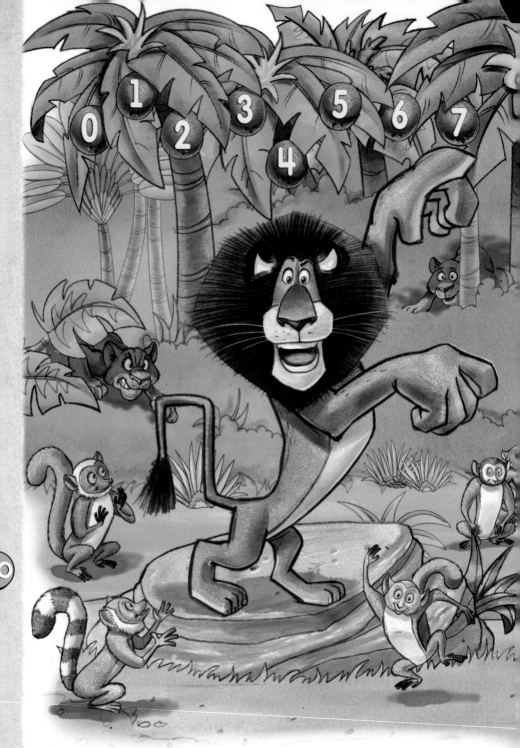

Alex performed at the watering hole. Marty and the locals cheered for him. It was just like home at the zoo! But hungry **fossa** were watching too.

8 9 10

Coconut Numbers

repeat

The penguins returned! They arrived just in time to save their zoo friends from the fossa.

1

2

GO

Penguin Memory

The four friends celebrated their last day together on Madagascar. Where will they go next?

African Music

repeat

25

A SNEAK PEEK...

DARE YOUR MOM TO TOUCH HERE!

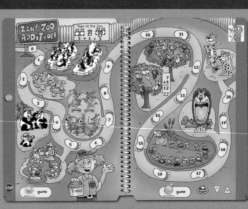

26

CHECK OUT
THE ENTIRE LIBRARY AT
WWW.LEAPFROG.COM
TO FIND THE PERFECT BOOK!

WITH CARDS!

Check out these other LeapPad™ books!

Kindergarten – 1st Grade

LeapPad™
Anna's First Ballet

K-1st Grade

Subject/skill
Reading Adventure

Teaches
• Ballet facts
• Introduction to French language
• Reading fluency
• Vocabulary
• Writing styles

Teaches
• Ballet facts
• Ballet positions
• French phrases
• Reading fluency
• Writing styles
• The Nutcracker

1st – 2nd Grade

LeapPad™
BUGS!
The Story of the Bug Wranglers

1st-2nd Grade

Subject/skill
Reading Adventure

Teaches
• Dozen of bug facts
• Science
• Vocabulary
• Reading fluency

Teaches
• Dozens of bug facts
• Science
• Vocabulary
• Reading fluency